Love Hotel

JANE UNRUE

Love Hotel

A NEW DIRECTIONS PAPERBOOK

Manufactured in the United States of America
New Directions Books are printed on acid-free paper.
First published as New Directions Paperbook 1299 in 2015
Design by Erik Rieselbach

Library of Congress Cataloging-in-Publication Data
Unrue, Jane.
Love hotel / by Jane Unrue. — First edition.
pages ; cm
ISBN 978-0-8112-2270-9 (softcover : acid-free paper)
1. Triangles (Interpersonal relations)—Fiction. I. Title.
PS3621.N65L69 2015
813'.6—dc23   2014027197

10 9 8 7 6 5 4 3 2 1

New Directions Books are published for James Laughlin
by New Directions Publishing Corporation
80 Eighth Avenue, New York 10011

Love Hotel

Day 1

Immediately striking was the silence
no faint music
low lighting inducing a feeling of
One morning a man and his wife were working in the hay.
I felt none of what I had imagined feeling before I left my apartment
building
none of what I felt when I got on the train.

Encased in frosted glass marked by a placard indicating no sign in requirements was the reception desk. The room selection panel resided in a dim corridor indicated by a freestanding sign to the left of the reception desk. As the guidebook explained some room selection panels display color photographs amenities the prices peak off peak. This was just a grid of numbered buttons lit ones vacant not too many vacants. Press it stick your card key falls card pops means time has come to leave behind the lobby.
I took the elevator
sweet perfume entwined in smoky men's cologne
up.

On the train I imagined that I was the woman sitting across from me. I have no memory of what this woman looked like what she was wearing what possessions she had with her on the train.

Right back into the elevator.

L

The man told his wife to climb up on the stack of hay.

After an unproductive stop at the room selection panel I slid my key under the reception desk window. Excuse me this room seems to be missing I said. A form appeared behind the frosted glass. I looked all over two but it's not there I said. The sound of sandy bottom shoes. Another key beneath the window.

So there's tile back there behind the reception desk I told myself.

New key in hand I passed the room selection corridor again.

Dark carpeting out here

embellished

3

the elevator closing

with an even darker pattern conveying a message that eyes might peek from underneath the pattern in the hope of catching someone's falling gaze.

On the train while imagining that I was the woman sitting across from me I slipped into a dream that I was in a country cottage taking care of a little boy. I don't know how old the boy was. I recall observing that although he was a little boy he seemed very small for his age. When I awoke due to a jolt experienced by the train the woman sitting across from me was looking straight into my eyes. I remember thinking: I know what you're thinking you're right under the circumstances there is no surprise in this.

What was truly shocking however was that the little boy in the dream I remember remembering

was not just small for his age he was downright tiny my eyes wandering to the train window as if I might see him careening white against the black sky. He was a boy whom I regarded as birdlike. He was not at any time in the dream a bird. As long as he was alive he was a boy the real point of the dream seeming to be that somehow this little boy had died in my arms his body having been transferred to a large heavy plate in my lap.

As a clock in the cottage slowly ticked I

midnight on the train

I watched the decomposing of the boy on the

noonday in the dream

blood

organs

flesh

The man disappeared into the field.

It was in response to their plea that my journey was initiated.

When a person who has not known suffering walks into a certain kind
of room she will be saddened shocked confused by what she feels
by what she *knows*
has happened there.

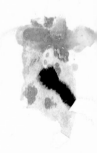

After a quick run through of my belongings I emerged from my
apartment building with my rolling suitcase tote bag other little things
that I might
matchbook in my hand
I was recalling information so ornately
irresistibly
The night we met he motioned to a padded chair said *Please sit down.*
He filled our glasses. Candles glowed expectantly. The air was crisp
the details intimately
mesmerizingly
the edges laced in black
black satin piping
jewel encrusted insects
black
adhered to
There's a spider
jewelbacked
on the
Now it's on the
Thus the story
white French netting
had begun.

A peanut butter sandwich candy muffin peanuts water notebook in my tote bag suitcase smartly packed it was already dark when the train pulled out of the station.

As soon as one layer of the little boy vanished the next layer vanished until eventually save the bones the tufts of hair the scatterings of dust no head there was not anything remaining on the plate.

I took the elevator right back down to L.

When I arrived at that hotel identified
It's one of those she whispered *where they go for just one night.*
as where to stay
their guidebook not at all insistent
Know what I mean? she whispered.
by a matchbook
instantly my feelings totally
Day Four: Having recently returned from walking to the CORNER
SOUTHMOST of their estate where once a tiny house had stood we
I felt so at home I knew that I could never get enough. I did not want
to leave. I could not even bear to think about a time when I would
were together on the VERANDAH.
When I got to that hotel however I stepped down into the patio protected by a wall of textured brick. A flagstone walkway curved around
a bed of flowers.
Filled with dread I tried to keep from seeing
hearing
There is someone in my room I repeated into the tiny opening in the
frosted glass window of the reception desk.
I mean to say I tried so hard to keep from being seen.
New key in hand I took the elevator up.

I'll try to trace this back to where it started from.

The night we met
One day a man and his wife
as I proceeded down their HALLWAY
SECOND FLOOR
then down their STAIRCASE
MAIN
were working in the
down the HALLWAY
GROUND FLOOR
passing three closed doors
I felt so homesick for my *bed*
my *windows*
floors
were working in the
even for my *walls*. But at the same time just as soon as I had seen them
seated in their STUDY I
We'd both completely understand he said to me when five nights later
we had moved to the VERANDAH where she said to me *If you feel
you can't do it*
When the night we met I saw them seated in the STUDY I felt more
at home than I had ever felt before. But previous to that moment I had
They were working in the hay.
As I proceeded down the HALLWAY
SECOND FLOOR I passed the door into their NURSERY
DAY. If I had gone inside the NURSERY
DAY then stepped into the
Had I innocently crossed the border from the one into the other then
I might have found a secret doorway to a tightly curling staircase
down into the GROUND FLOOR corner of their KITCHEN
terminating on their BASEMENT floor.
You see
We'd both completely understand.

the night we met they took me out to their estate.

They took me in their mansion.

Led me up the STAIRCASE

NORTH

up to the SECOND FLOOR where all the bedrooms were. *We have two nurseries up here too* he said. *Connected from inside.* He pointed to a door. Explaining that attaching to the NURSERY

DAY was

No there was not any hallway door into the NURSERY

NIGHT. The only way to get into the NURSERY

NIGHT was if you entered through

He said *But you won't need to go in there.*

Across the hall then down a bit she opened up a door into a pretty lemon yellow

sitting room connected to a bathroom. She said *When you've freshened up*

Come down he interrupted.

You can find us in the study she said.

Fourth door on the left he said.

Her eyes however indicated that she would not understand at all.

I can't!

He first considers turning walking straight into the park but then considers turning back to where he started.

No!

Nor will he

He

There is a lake within the park a platform for a band raised terrace lined with statues. Platform leads by pathway to a small pavilion circled by stone pedestalled containers filled with

blood red

yellow

dark wine woven

He

who shall be introduced a little later on

continues walking.

autumn flowers

bone white

head cracked open

First I saw the flashing. Then I heard a giggling. Noted that the
flashing came from sequins disappearing through the automatic doors
when I stepped down into the patio as soon as I arrived at that hotel.
I walked along the flagstone walkway curved around a flowerbed
then stepping down again I entered through the automatic doors.
Nobody there. I found the room selection panel chose a room got in
the elevator
2
vibrations of a sparkling woman with a silent man who as she stepped
into the elevator held his hand against her back as if to lead her gently
into there.
I got out of the
They were working in the hay.
walked right
left
got back in the
L
again
Excuse me this room seems to be—
new key
back in it
3
again
again
turned right
stuck in the
HEY! GET—!
down again to
There is someone in my room I said into the tiny opening in
The man told his wife to climb up on the stack.
In other words when I arrived I couldn't tell whom I had seen when I
saw flashing.

The man told his wife to stamp it down with her pitchfork.
Yet another key in hand I took the elevator up.
The man
It isn't what you think it is I should have told the woman sitting
opposite me on the train.
the field
Some dreams are just about plates I should have said. Instead I had
looked out the window of the train recalling the crisp clean pattern of
blue edging the rim.
The man disappeared into the

1. *Was there any indication that you were leaving?*
2. *Was there something we should have seen or done?*

Prepared to log
survey
the contents
607
I recalled another question to be asked of him
by me
for
I mean on behalf of
the event of running into
*3. Did you say anything or did you do anything that we should have
picked up on?*
this question followed by a secondary question that would predict-
ably be asked
of me
by him.
We pulled up to the station. I got out with all of my belongings. She
rolled down the window. She said *If I know him as I think I know him*
I could feel his presence in the atmosphere around the station but I
could not feel his presence on the train or when I got to that hotel.
She said *He'll ask you this.*

There was a lady with a face of white
limbs white
white hair. She wore a regal gown of heavy silver white brocade the fitted bodice following her figure featuring at the top a neckline framed in lace with coral satin scooped to flatter. Short capped sleeves. Peg pleat on either side the central opening in her skirt revealed the underskirts of coral inset with a rosepoint lace with sequins rhinestones pearls. A sweeping train made possible by the fullness of the skirt was drawn into a bustle in the back the waistline of the bodice catching up into a bow. The bow was flat. In time the dress would yellow
then
Don't think her hard or cruel. The lady is
was
good kind gentle only lacking in a talent for
She had an aptitude for saving people not however for the
She had taken on as protégée had stopped from suicide no less a seamstress with a child. All that the seamstress had possessed a painting of a basket on a table pomegranate grapes an apple peach two perfect grape leaves hovering over one more apple pear quince one more peach was given to the lady who immediately arranged to have it hung in her boudoir. The lady gave the seamstress sleeping quarters put her under the authority of her chambermaid then found her neverending piles of work with several of her wealthiest acquaintances. The seamstress lived she worked inside the lady's home her child beside her at her
left
right
Most unfortunately though the lady whom we yet may picture as a flitting snow white figure with a sparkling coral inset was oblivious to the sad conditions under which the seamstress had to work her child to pass his hours on top of hours engaged in only those most compact most restrictive forms of playing.
For example he imagined himself as hovering in each corner of the ceiling

floor

The chambermaid had put the seamstress in

At other times he saw himself as hanging from a thread's length down a wall.

a type of linen storage closet used for sewing now. In winter under insufficient light the only heating issued from a little stove polluting the air from morning on. The seamstress who was very grateful to her benefactress did not ever make complaints. She kept her child beside her far enough away from in that unforgiving space the terrible stove as best she could.

The child who although he was very young when he had seen it would it seemed not ever forget the night when after mother had released his hand he watched her climb onto the bridge's railing stand there weeping into dawn's first glimmer when the lady suddenly appeared accelerated screamed for her to *Wait!* So there

were no complaints from child. At least not for a

Stop!

There's more. The lady had a woman brought into the house. She was an elderly woman who had lost her family lost her friends was at the brink herself. The charitable lady kept the elderly woman working long beyond the days when most employers would have let her go. She did not realize just how overworked the poor old woman who had never asked for anything had been. She did not understand the deep fatigue. Depression. Nightmares. Searching. Did not even know that when the elderly woman's workday up down basement stairs had started in out attic spaces cellar storage places bathrooms cloakrooms

she

the lady

though she never thought of it like this

she still had three four hours to go within her overstuffed deep buttoned rose boudoir with salmon accents on the cushions carpets curtain tassels vanity seat. As she slept soundly underneath a scarlet coverlet all contact with the world at work remained suspended.

He said *It is just that there is no one else possessing what you*
We both said so just as soon as we first saw you standing there she
interrupted.
Clearly they could see in me what others had not seen in me
that in me all impressions feelings touches multiply
I told him she's the one she said.
solidify
He said *That's what she said to me.*

Take hold of me.

Day Four: She looked me in the eye as if to share a secret. He looked well beyond us toward the NORTH FAÇADE. We stood upon a patch of land on the estate within the CORNER SOUTHMOST where a tiny house once stood. The stonework for that tiny house as he explained was laid by local masons. He said *Quarried locally* then told us that a boat was bought to carry the stone down river. *All of this was engineered* he said *by him.*
He means the late great Milton Butterfield she said.

Day Five: We then began the long walk back
To the VERANDAH she had said.
It was a period of remarks about the grounds the foliage seasons
winter coming Christmas presents apple cider holly berry satin
ribbon. I looked out across the lawn that seemed in its expansiveness
to validate my sudden dreading of the weeks the days until it would
be Christmas Day. As we approached the rising slope to where THE
FIVE STONE STEPS would take us to the walkway hooking
around the CORNER
NORTHWEST of the mansion she said *Now just getting back to
what we had been talking about last night*
She paused.
I turned to watch a twinkling snowfall taking place across the lawns.
Black birds were diving skipping leaving coal black markings on the
white. Then suddenly
excruciatingly
the snow
the markings
disappeared.
The CORNER
NORTHWEST had bay windows looking out upon an autumn
colors view that reached down to the boathouse.
Be prepared I told myself. They're going to ask you something you
won't want to answer with an answer.
I peeked in the window from outside.

607

I stuck the key into the

Covering all four walls a figurative print rich brilliant colors created a selection of the principal trades chief occupations aspects of the Chinese style of life. Against a dark red background illustrated cutouts of a rural Chinese landscape featured brightly colored Chinese figures firing pots they hauled the pots away they loaded them on the junk they gathered rice stacked rice they argued to a judge they carried out the various stages in production not just tea but silk they even grew a Chinese garden.

It was papered in a weighty dense repetitive unceasing world of working. Talking.

Thinking.

Still it was a cheerful although seedy room small lamps on either side of the *bed* a Chinese chandelier two floor lamps plus a table lamp without its shade *bed* covered with a leafy *bedspread* bearing no stylistic similarity even to the garden illustrations on the *walls*. The *bed* was big enough for two coordinated with a red gold wingback *chair* set in the corner near the *window*. *Bed* like *chair* was decorated with gold satin *pillows* differing in their shapes all old all floppy threadbare looking.

Then I

Yes I would have liked to get to business but I took my boots off closed the heavy *curtains* peeled the *bedspread* back exposing

Once there were two teenaged sons who on cool moonlit evenings left their home and walked into the woods presumably to court young girls.

a pale pink

When I thought I saw a moving form behind the glass he took me gently by the arm then turned us all around to face the autumn colors view said *There look back down there.* He motioned with his finger toward the east. *Now following the slope down to that tree* he said *you should be able to catch the corner of the boathouse there.*

She said *We'll take you there.*

Of course we'll take her there he said.

She said *We'll have a picnic by the boathouse.*

Though I wanted to I did not ask them when the picnic would take place.

In time the shock will fade. Her sadness may diminish too. Although
repeated entrances
new acts of waking
walls the softest blue
may give impressions of repeated shock
soft carpet
blue
gauze curtains shimmering in the night
each shock remains as freshly devastating
undulating
heart
knees
fingers
as the old shock was.

No it was not my intention to fall asleep. It was my intention to rest my eyes get up go look for him.

Day 2

Next morning due to (Room Service: N) to (Restaurant: N) to
(Vending Machines: N) (Coffee/Tea: N) I went out to find a place for
breakfast.

*Late one night concealing himself behind a tree their father who for
various reasons had become suspicious of these outings watched his sons
begin to roll upon the ground beside a campfire.*

After breakfast I walked back through playground in the park through
park then made the rest of the way to the hotel. I went up to my room
collected (Bag Storage: N) then took the elevator right back down
returned the key into the slot below the room selection panel.

*In this clearing lit up by the fire beneath a heavy to bursting moon the
sons rolled over and over becoming as their father watched them wolves.*

Besides some unexplainable sounds a shaving smell or two the
hallways whiff of mouthwash breath were empty. If not for so few
illuminated numbers on the room selection grid I would have sworn
all rooms were empty too. The place felt empty
although utterly full of
I don't think he's here I just don't think this thing is right I told myself
when I stepped out into the patio began to make my way to (Recommended: Y).

A week

I think

It's hard to say. No depth. No clear perspective. No free space.

before I met them I had started having problems with my

Previously

But this had been my pattern for as long as

sleep.

A lack of evidence.

I woke up. Walked. Discovered I was in the light of the refrigerator

opening up a little tub of

Just about a week before I met them though I found that I would wake

up get up out of bed

dried cherries. Not so interested anymore in snacks I found that I was

walking through my dark apartment

As their father watched them from behind the trees the wolves attacked

and murdered a couple walking on the rarely traveled footpath.

to a hanging photograph from which I

When I met them for about a week or more before that meeting I had

started hearing wheezing coughing sobbing squeezing out the corners

of the frame. I'd turn around walk back get into bed return to sleep

wake up walk back to it again.

The night we met my sleeping troubles disappeared.

Night Five: *A bit more wine girls?* he said.

We were seated on the VERANDAH.

Be right back he said.

She leaned in closer to me said *It seems as though we have a deep connection you and I. Do you know what I mean?*

Night Six: We said goodbye just at the edge of the estate where parked beside the gate a taxicab was waiting in the dark.

Night Seven: After getting ready after giving my bags a run through guidebook matchbook I emerged from my apartment building right on schedule having factored in the likely waiting time for taxicabs around the corner by the bus stop. Right away I noticed that their car was sitting out in front of my apartment building. I had not expected them to pick me up

especially after what had happened on the night before

but

Hurrying my approaching I

especially after what

She stuck her head out of the car as if to say *Surprise.*

I got into their car. I had the feeling I was leaving behind a swarm.

Let's go she said.

but

Yes let's get me out of here I told myself.

I exited the Public Library (Restaurant: N) with (Bag Storage: N) but (Restrooms: Y) with all of my belongings with me. Then I ducked into the market just across the street. I had decided I would eat my lunch at one of the little wrought iron tables in the tree lined fairly crowded park behind the Public Library. Tourists mainly local couples working people baby strollers.

After another long much longer stint inside the (Recommended: Y) I went back over to the market spooned up dinner from the buffet of prepared foods set into a wide bank of warming trays before stopping at the adjacent drugstore. Fear of awakening in the middle of the night without sufficient

Weaving in among the trees the father hurried home while praying that his children who as far as he could tell were ignorant of his watching them would choose the easier slower path back to the house.

I bought some extra snacks because I was afraid of waking up to nothing next to me to eat.

Sky darkening the air a little chilly

There's a suffocating feeling that I get when clouds roll in.

I stepped into the patio then down again to enter through the automatic doors.

You might not turn up anything she said.

I chose a number. Then

As if the clouds are rolling right into my mouth

And that's why we need you he later said.

I took the elevator up.

my nose

the space behind my eyes

I feel

I feel

It seemed as if the darkness was what pulled that train along as if the darkness pulled the train to just exactly where it wanted all the people in the train with all their things to go.

The lady
more like vapor these days seeping through the cracks between the
floorboards or through gaps around the door
grew somehow conscious of what heavy burdens these two women
one who had a child
However on her own she couldn't possibly have
He
The child
Although he did one day become
It was a frigid day when memories of the night his mother climbed
releasing him from her grasp up to the railing on the bridge began to
dim. He was a young man now who thanks to just one gentle request
from mother to the chambermaid
The chambermaid was happy to help a child whose eyes she often
thought showed true compassion
empathy
extraordinary sympathy resulting from a limitless sensitivity to
capacity for
To look into his eyes she told the lady when appealing in the child's
behalf is first to lose yourself inside their color then you find that
you've come out upon the other side confronted by a trail into a forest
of unfathomable dimension. Depth. So little sky. Those eyes.
So many trees.
He thus began to get his lessons in the mornings with the children
from a nearby mansion. As he grew he more repeatedly began to think
of nothing other than revenge for not just all the years his delicately
featured fragile little mother spent inside that closet but for how her
time on earth had bottomed out.

When on the train awakened by a jolt I
Slipping back into my country cottage dream I started to anticipate
the return of the little boy's parents. Absent from the dream they were
apparently returning to the cottage. I grew anxious then
The rimmed in small blue painted flowers plate was trembling on my
lap.
about what in the world I could say to the two familiar
They looked so familiar in that dream.
familiar figures who would all too soon be standing in the cottage
doorway conjoined in a shared expression of knowing parental terror
glazed over with a rapidly disappearing layer of hope. How can I
possibly explain this thing I asked myself about the plate.
I awakened again. All quiet save the sounds of the train. Through the
window I could watch the sky. The moon was full. I did not look at
the woman sitting across from me. I only thought about the dream.

The answer that they
We were in the ENTRANCE
MAIN
(Night Five)
which as he pointed out
You have to admit he said.
was high. A gabled
pretty impressive!
stone projection to the right side of the STAIRCASE
MAIN
The answer was that he had disappeared before.
I felt as though I
Having spent my lifetime tangled up in skeins of thinnest threads I felt
as though at last I was beginning to unweave.
Except he always
Sometimes it can take a few days she said. *Even weeks* he said.
came home.
She said *However this time seems a little*
That's why we need you he interrupted. He was looking up into the
ceiling.
She was looking down.

I stuck the key into the

402

It was a double with an ivory eyelet canopy on top with ruffle around
the bottom both in dusty pink coordinated loosely with the *carpet* more
directly with the *walls* all painted in the same pink color. Not just one
but two gold painted *chairs* pink *cushions* shared a cozy corner with a
floor lamp near a tripod table bunch of artificial flowers in a vase. The
lightness of the *carpet* with the shortness of the ruffle meant that every
corner of the room could be looked into even underneath the *bed*.
There was a blocked off *fireplace* white painted *grate* the *window*
dressed in triple treatment of white vinyl blind behind a gauzy dark
green *curtain* fringed at top with matching valance. May sound good
but it was seedy. A little dirty. Worse than 607. There were pictures
though. A row of slightly banged up seasonal depictions of a lake
a seated conversation on a porch two different sailing scenes one
ordinary sailing scene one showing children using sticks to push toy
boats across the surface of a pond. But catching my attention in a
lingering way
It started with a jolt.
was one medium sized portrait
good condition
hung above the *fireplace*.

If we should try imagining the raw intensity of the feelings of that
child
a man now
we would find a new example of
The child became a
uncontrolled connection with not one
not two
He waits.
He walks.
He passes fluidly among three states of consciousness.

I laid a towel across the *bed*. I opened the spaghetti suddenly remembering after buttering the bagel halves a dream from several nights ago that I had not recalled until the moment when I stepped into the train. On board I passed from car to car looked for a seat across from seats still empty. When I spotted just exactly what I wanted I remembered dreaming of

I felt a momentary pang of longing sitting eating on the *bed*.

All dark. As I could suddenly recall on board that train the person in the dream who chased me was unknown. While being chased while crossing from the concrete walkway to the grass while trying desperately to keep my distance out in front I also tried while crossing grass to walkway grass to slow my shifting sense of who he was. This effort to arrest his image as the high speed nature cameras capture

for example

wingbeats

Not a moment to explain the horrors to his wife not even to describe the bride's

white

fur

handwarmer

torn to shreds

the lightly traveled pathway sprinkled with a curly bloody mess

diagonally the man cut through the clearing opened up the door and grabbed his wife and told her that they had to leave at once because their sons were coming home.

This wanting to identify the man was

Drawing a halt to this accelerating period of remembering was a woman on the train who sat across from me. I had no memory of her physical appearance or possessions but I vividly remembered some of what

This wanting to identify the man was overtaken by the physical necessity in seeing my apartment building stop itself from smearing blurring fading fast because of being chased around so rapidly repeatedly by us.

a couple of the woman's thoughts.

It now occurred to me that this might be a good occasion to review take stock of things I'd done things not done things I'd seen or speculated even playing back my

I will finish dinner take a rest then go back up to 6 then down to 3 to have a look around I told myself.

The first real difference
he explained
(Night Five)
the three of us still standing in the ENTRANCE
MAIN
was in the phone calls. Starting two days after they had seen him for
the last time day or night at least one phone call came. Nobody spoke
no sound no numbers visible on the caller identification screen.
Gradually they noticed the duration of the calls decreasing. At the
same time it became more troubling to receive one. She especially had
found these calls from no name calling from no number so upsetting
that he had requested that if she could not see
He said *Any numbers on the*
I agreed immediately she interrupted.
Our discussion of this subject was confined entirely to the
ENTRANCE
MAIN.

49

A birdcage hung behind her. By her feet there was a little wild eyed dog that although seated clearly saw himself as runner digger upper. She did not look shy though in her face particularly in the way her eyes appeared to gaze into the eyes of someone something just behind the painter. There was in her bearing true respectability. The room in which she posed a cheerful parlor with a window casting light onto the birdcage bars looked busy although stationary. Crowded. Costly. It was typical of the kinds of portraits meant to celebrate a life of privilege not accompanied by an unappealing temperament. However paired with all this pleasantness there was if one knew where to look mysteriousness. Her dress was gray with mauve the roses giving off a hint of something lurking in the shadows of the folds. Up near her shoulder was a brooch depicting in a silhouette a long haired male or female profile every facet of the brooch edged delicately in the tiniest purple gemstones. On the wall behind the birdcage was a roughly detailed drawing of a child. To see this portrait of a woman was to feel compelled to turn look over one's own shoulder then to turn again look closely at the child.

Canary in a cage.

The *fireplace grate.*

I was awakened by a shrill distressing sound. A cry.
Then falling again into a kind of
One night when the moon was full a girl was taken away to a lagoon.

As I was nodding off I
Once again I slipped

*Her naked body first was painted red then decorated thoroughly with
yellow lines white dots and on her head she wore a sacred ceremonial
object fashioned out of sticks.*

I heard a crash. Door slamming. Stomps. Another crash.

Some noises are almost impossible to trace much less interpret. I decided to rely on my first understanding of the cry: distressing sound. I
could not say if it had come through *wall* or *ceiling*

floor. I just looked over at the clock. I waited for another one to come.

The second most important difference she explained
the three of us still standing in the ENTRANCE
MAIN
between this last time and the other times before
While I expected I would feel her hand slip into mine I did not feel it.
*was the feeling all throughout not just the house throughout the whole
estate as soon as he had left.*

The road becoming gloomier
instead of heading to the park he nonetheless advances certain that he
took a wrong turn somewhere.
Where?
Impossible for him to understand such unkind limitation total desolation deep despondency heart racing panic tempered by a head to toe
exhaustion making a mess of his interior conversation part in pictures
partway uttered
swallowed up by breaths that he can almost see
It's getting cold.
he feels that he is dropping to his knees
What's doing this?
right on the sidewalk right there on the
No not there!
but he's not stopping
has continued walking
flying
tipping
feeling of a body shackled by a paralyzing arm or neck injection lying
motionless enclosed within a body that cannot stop moving
Has to get there.
walking
Has to go.

The night we met we all went back to their estate. It was an invitation
I accepted gladly even though I have a policy against accepting rides
when I am working.

It was long. They had been talkative at first but things got quiet as the
way grew darker sending us into something far more rural

You have questions?

deeper.

When I first began to see the narrowing of his eyes in

Is he falling

Is this whole car falling

glimpses of the rearview mirror I began to dare myself to take increas-
ingly longer looks into the mirror

disappearing eyes

I

Am I going down or is it is it possible that I am actually going

Yes my dear I will endeavor to tell you everything I know.

It was the turn onto a gravel road that woke me up.

We entered through the gate continuing on the gravel drive until we
parked.

I nearly could remember something someone said.

We got out stood there looking. Much too dark to see their home with
any kind of clarity but I could feel that it was massive. I could sense the
deep impression of despondency was lessening within me. At the same
time I confirmed a certain blackness swelling from inside. I looked back
at the car then followed them into what he called the ENTRANCE
NOT THE MAIN ONE.

Turning back to look again I thought I saw a figure seated in the
backseat of that car.

Impossible.

Impossible I told myself.

He said *You first*.

We started up the STAIRCASE
MAIN.

Then came the other cry.

The girl who had been decorated held a sharpened bone in each one of her hands.

Another crash. Wind hitting at the *window*.

I looked at the clock got out of *bed* turned on the floor lamp put my coat on boots stepped out into the hallway when a man was passing by.

I wanted so to turn look at the man

Don't look at him.

but I did not as I was certain of his turning looking back at me.

I heard him exiting into a room at the other end of the hall

the high ceilinged corridor only barely lit by sconces two of which were out.

Listening briefly I

I then was under the impression that he was a gray man rigid walker scented pipe tobacco peppermints cologne.

I listened at the

404

Then

403

At last with arms extended up bones glowing in the moonlight she who had been painted yellow white and red began to sing.

The stonework he explained *was laid by local masons. Quarried locally* he said. *A boat was bought to carry it down the*
We will take you there she interrupted *just as soon as*
Yes we will he said.

It was a shimmering late fall afternoon when we began our walk back to the mansion from the CORNER
SOUTHMOST of the property where once a tiny house had stood. We crossed a sweeping wide expanse of land a type of beauty I had never before
But yet I felt so desperately familiar to the point of gnawing trepidation with the things that I was seeing as if I had been anticipating every glimpse each word all happenings. As we walked northward toward the mansion save occasionally inserted bits of information about the mansion the estate our conversation was devoted to the planning of a picnic by the river. It was paradise. A side effect however was that this short walk would plant in me mysteriously concentrated notions of regret spun round by uncontrolled anxiety for what was on its way.

Aboard the train within that little country cottage time slowed time leaped forward tailing back anticipation dread in tandem working to postpone to speed the heartbreaking eventuality in the form of two dark figures standing faceless in the doorway backlit by a sunset fully ablaze.

Awakened yet again I got out of the *bed*.

This really is too much I told myself.

You might not turn up anything she had told me with an ambivalence
that showed quite plainly in her face as if an invisible line protected
the upper fearing portion from the hoping part below. He had no such
divisions. *If you see anything that makes you nervous* he insisted *call us*.

I put on my coat my boots picked up my key went out into the hallway just in time to see a man emerging from the elevator. It was dark
down there.

Don't look.

I think it was a robe but could have been a coat. He turned around.

Don't let him think you noticed him.

What launched his getting back into the elevator was a glance at me. I
indicated to this man that he was not where he belonged. Unless the
man was merely trying to avoid me. If to see me meant *wrong floor* to
him then

whether below

above

I told myself

he must be staying

vertically

that is

in

302

the same room as my

502

Unless

I told myself

he's staying in the room next door

Unless

which

404

61

Regardless

Seeing me was something that the man had wanted to avoid. If that is true I told myself then I am likely onto something here.

I hurried back into my room where the unexpected sight of my tote bag pocketbook along with other little bags all loaded on the *chair* my coat draped over it convinced me to leave the floor lamp on for the rest of the night.

But then one blustery day the calls began to

Concerning the calls they had received since he had disappeared
there was a new development about which only one of them was

Then the calls started to change he said to me.

Night Four: We stood within the ENTRANCE

BUSINESS

underneath the taller narrower gable left of ENTRANCE

MAIN.

Originally built he said *for secret access to and from the study.*

She had gone to check on dinner. He was there with me alone.

So this is how it is I told myself. The three of us. The smell of dinner.

Rest of the world be damned.

According to his story she away for weekend errands he home wash-
ing dishes tidying up a bit

Staff's off on weekends he had (Night One) told me.

Night Four: when the phone rang. This most recent call he answered
from this no one calling them from nowhere was a call about which he
decided not to tell her.

But I'm telling you he said. I thought I felt his leg approaching mine.

This time unlike the other times there was a noise in the receiver.

Hey you two she called out from the STUDY

door popped open showing us a tempting glimpse into the STUDY

I've been looking everywhere for you.

She often asks herself how she can best receive these sentiments of
deep affiliation that attempt to reach her from she knows not where.
She's deeply conscious of the sender but she cannot reach the sender.
Therefore she has nothing to do but wait inside this room
all blue
all patternings
varieties of undulation.
Feelings that had once been shock now float about her like a galaxy of
silver dots.

Day 3

Next morning exiting through the automatic doors then crossing through the patio to take the two steps up into the little ivy covered archway I was for the second time confronted with the vision of abandoned businesses across the street. However on that dreary morning those uneven overhangs doors windows boarded painted overpostered mismatched signs seemed oddly unified.
We have a favor to ask you she had said.
How could I find someone in such a place as this I asked myself. When staying in the patio for any length of time to see who comes who goes is not an option. Same for watching from across the street. Instead of going out for breakfast I had waited out the morning rain repacking polishing off my snacks. Now headed back to (Recommended: Y) I felt so disappointed. Worried. Even fearful. I was wondering if this whole trip wasn't just a serious underestimation of the challenges in finding someone who so clearly
On my left the drugstore then the market suddenly I realized
Public Library at my back
I found that I had turned the corner going in a new

I walked. I headed in a new
She said *I just can't tell you what this means to me.*
I walked.
He said *To us.*
Until I stopped. I checked the guidebook. Started toward the concrete ramp.

Divided into thirds by swooping golden banisters the massive staircase had been made entirely avoidable by the presence of the concrete
ramp off to its left.

I rolled my suitcase up to enter through the double doors then
followed the sign to where I checked my (Bag Storage: Y) then stuffed
my other things inside a (Lockers: Y) before I got into the nonmem-
bers line for (Family/Senior/Group Rates: Y).

But are you absolutely certain that they don't know where I am?

The evening when this journey first began I felt no little trepidation for the task that I was taking on. However as I went through my belongings one last time despite the guidebook's lack of anything encouraging to say about it I imagined my accommodations as a small oasis respite from a life that I had wanted for so long to find a way to Grateful for the circumstances that had like a miracle

Because you can anticipate the needs of other living forms you also understand the need for sacrifice.

It came to me that I

And in acknowledgment of this you're being handsomely

I was convinced that finally I had received the opportunity to have the sort of

find a way

She said *We knew it just as soon*

Indeed as we approached the station as the distance from the swarm increased as light accumulated bit by bit around the car as we got closer to the place for pulling over at the station taking up the empty seat beside me in the car I started to imagine him for whom I would be searching sitting there when we would all be riding back to the estate the four of us together in the car.

We just can't tell you how much we

However when I got on board that train I was reminded of a pairing of environments

two worlds that must remain apart

a powerful relationship

He said *It's true.* He said *You really are.*

blue skies

green rolling hills

a glittering wavy line across the broad horizon.

She said *She knows what she is.*

White puffy clouds above

bright flashing colors down below.

When I arrived at that hotel the feeling that I had was even more unsettling. Jesus God what am I doing here I asked myself. That night I tried to call them but they did not answer it.

They did not ever answer any of my calls again.

Although the guidebook clearly noted quite a few
(Successive Nights: N) (Restaurant: N) (Bar: N)
potential inconveniences
before arriving
Know what I mean?
I thoroughly anticipated seeing people in the elevator
hallways
going in
out
waiters maybe maids at least
not only fleeting shadows
flashes
Man 1
2
I pictured couples meeting talking waiting (Smoking: Y) reclining in
the (Lobby Seating: N).
It's true. The lobby wasn't much. No telephones no cubbyholes no
wingback chairs.
I'll try to trace this back to where it started from again.

The night we met I did not stay the night. They had me driven home by taxicab. As we progressed along the rural roads the city glowing up ahead I watched a gently broken playback of the night. When I awakened due to our arrival at my building I remember looking at the rearview mirror for the taxi driver's eyes. I have no memory of the taxi driver's eyes. It was as if the taxi driver had no face.

I fully wanted to expect that on the following Friday I would turn around at work to see them sitting there again. But when that Friday came they were not there.

BETWEEN THE NEXT TWO WEEKS I frequently discovered I had slipped into a halfway dreaming state in which I walked inside a tunnel. I would stop hold up a candle to the tunnel walls as if in search of something on or in the walls.

You see the night we met they took me back to their estate. *To our place* as he called it. Then *Our generous conspicuously simple main roof used as dominating background to a sequence of assorted minor themes.* I freshened up went down the STAIRS turned left passed three closed doors. They got up from their heavy leather chairs as soon as I appeared within the doorway to the STUDY. On the wall above the fireplace above a little lacquered box that sat off center on the mantel near an oval mirror on a pewter stand there hung a photographically realistic painting of a house. As viewed through open gates it was a small but sumptuous symmetrically arranged stone manor with a front façade encrusted with carved flowers complemented by stone pots that lined the bottom edge containing living flowers of the same variety as the carved ones.

That's another one of his he said.

A black front door. Bright doorknob. Knocker. Disc shaped window up above the knocker. Those same flowers set like handprints in the glass. Then two weeks later when I turned around at work to see them in their usual spot I felt that something I had been so desperate for in order to survive had been administered to my soul. I also felt that I had known that this would be the night although this sense of knowing did not lessen my relief at seeing them. That night (Night Two) my shift completed we went back to their estate. When we arrived they led me to the DRAWING ROOM where following champagne with several chunks of chocolate almond bark the invitation came to stay the night. Although at first I hesitated

Don't do anything to show premeditation.

I accepted. When they led me up to where the bedrooms were she opened up the door into the pretty lemon sitting room connected to a bathroom. She said *Since you are familiar with it you can stay in here.* She opened up another door to show me that connected to the sitting room there was a pale orange rose pink bedroom that I had not seen the last time. She said *You'll find everything you need in there.* So after freshening up I joined them briefly in the STUDY. Next we went to the VERANDAH where he pointed to a padded chair said *Please.* She said *Sit down.* He said *I'll get some wine.* She said she had a story to tell me.

After that I did not see them for three weeks.

BETWEEN THE WEEKS my sleeping went uninterrupted although in the dreamlike spaces of my waking life when I was not examining the tunnel with the candle I began to see collected pictures fused together into overlays that covered up the real life version of the world. Blank surfaces were most susceptible. Some not blank surfaces turned blank when I had looked at them which made them ready to be filled with pictures. IN THESE WEEKS my sleep began to change as well. Although as soon as I had met them all my sleeping troubles disappeared

no waking walking to that photograph at which I listened for the wheezing coughing sighing trapped behind the glass

I here began to find that in the morning I would wake up crying as though having suddenly recalled a tragedy that seamless sleep had temporarily screened out. In tears my body trembling in my bed I looked around the room. Upon the *surfaces* the *objects* all the *fabrics* even on the *walls* I made out traces of a presence. None of the details. Just the loss.

INSIDE OF THOSE THREE WEEKS I had decided that if given the chance to do it I would stay the weekend although so as not to give the wrong impression

Do not let them think you're overeager.

So I told myself that I would not say yes immediately. The night they showed up in their usual spot my heart skipped beats inside my body that was strangely enough relaxed. I felt like lying down. I also had a boundless energy to be expended. When my shift was done we left together. We were getting in the car when she requested that I stay the weekend. How she asked it sealed my certainty about the wisdom in accepting. Doubtless I was entering into something that had weathered generations. Stabilized by rules of etiquette refined by deep felt understandings of propriety of decency of wholesomeness this shape was fixed then fortified against the changing times by surface over surface of the way that things had always been laid down in alternation with the way that things should always be. He never joined us in the conversation about the weekend but as soon as I accepted he said *Great.* They drove me to my building waiting in the car while I went in to gather everything that I would need from my apartment.

It was very late when I awakened when we turned onto the gravel road on their estate. We all went straight upstairs. This room was different from the last room. This new room was situated farther down the hall beyond a little antique bookcase then around the corner where beside the door there was an antique lyre back chair that clearly was not meant for sitting on. I went to bed immediately. My sleeping was not interrupted. Following that I did not see them for a month.

She does not tremble although recently she finds herself entirely
overcome by feelings
more like waves
of desolation
patterns
of anticipation.
Waiting for she knows not what she takes her clothes off.
Opens up her case.
Selects the things that she will need.
Takes out a candle.
Lights it.

I stepped through the doorway to the stately hall of statues Roman
Greek an elevated grand arrangement of cracked heroes
chipped
their bodies turned in different directions
heads
the ones that had them
angled differently
the faces pointed at a variety of spots well in the distance of that
limited although eternally unknowable majestic city. Their gaze was
collective
fixed as by coordinated effort on a set of points beyond those parch-
ment tinted walls. Effect of having eyeholes rather than real eyes I told
myself. Their expressions possessing vacancy as well as depth each
searing cold stone look was trained upon a destination far too distant
formless timeless for the living seeing person even to envisage.

My first night in that hotel
If I could clarify
If I could just
I woke up put my coat on boots went out into the hallway listened
605
but I heard nothing save the distant rumble of the ice machine. I
wondered what would bring a person to a place like this.
There's something going on in there I told myself. The elevator
seemingly modern but so noisy kicking into motion sent me hurrying
back into my
607
clarify if I
That night although I
On that night it's true I nodded off almost immediately. But later on I
did wake up. I had a hard time pulling
Once awakened
drink of water
snacks
I could not get to sleep again. My gaze was totally unwilling to abandon that one portion of the ceiling where strange sinewy reflections
had begun emerging from the areas closest to the Chinese chandelier.
This final question concerning what they knew
did not
But are you absolutely certain that they
to be asked by him as a predicted answer to the questions asked by
me for
Was there
Was there
had inspired in me not just contemplation. I was getting nervous.
Feeling hungry too.
I got up out of bed put on my coat my boots then
key

I stepped into the hallway listening
605
but hearing nothing I went back into my
607
water
snacks
I closed my eyes but still I saw those shimmering squiggling shapes.
They seemed to spill out from the center of my mind.

Regardless of his current state or his location he began to find himself transported back into that closet looking down upon the little seam-stress down below.

The child

a young man now sent off to school

as from a hovering point of view deriving from an upper corner spot was tiny enough that she his mother who was graceful light methodi-cally at work upon a purple gown of heavy satin with a pattern of gold peacock plumes was ignorant of his presence. He could see within the purple gown a golden wildness into which he could have dropped himself although he also saw among the golden eyes within the pattern overwhelming possibilities for not just weeping rivers but for sending out a multitudinous unyielding one eyed mesmerizing stare back at the world.

Upon a dreadful morning she had floated high upon a bridge however now she lived inside a closet dedicated to a gown that would precede another gown another gown another until one day when she was working diligently on a sheer white silk chiffon

the neckline of the bodice square in front

V shape in back

just like a story

gathering of the finest ecru lace to frame the neckline

split in two:

1. seamstress who was rescued from a railing
2. little mother drowning in the icy depths below

the bodice heavily embroidered with a silk floss goldenrod design outlined with silver thread through crystal beads the straight skirt flared just slightly at the hemline flowing into a sweeping train origi-nating at the hip.

Perhaps it was the future that revealed itself to him all splattered across the goldenrod design traced through the skirt increasing in a heavier pattern of embellishment as it approached the

splattered on the
No mere hemline it was nothing less than an inevitable explosion of
gold crystal beads among gold sparkling rhinestone studs
Not just embellishment
all splattered too.
The hip.
The hip.
Unable to endure this he would pray to be transported elsewhere.
Where?

The fact that I could check or lock my coat my suitcase tote bag everything I carried made the City Museum quite well suited to my situation. In addition to a fancy glass walls (Restaurant: Y) there was a central courtyard entered through a (Cafeteria: Y). I brought my tray into the (Outdoor Seating: Y) to eat among the families tourists locals mostly there in pairs except for elderly people who like velum cutouts flapped at times almost invisible in shifting autumn light. The galleries the corridors so crowded
everywhere
filled up
then layered over
all those faces
buried under
peeking out
I was so desperate to get out of there the whole time I was there.

Come here.

WITHIN THAT MONTH I took an unexpected course of action
that although a little reckless shocking quietly it had presented itself
to me as simply unavoidable. It happened three weeks in when I went
home from work. Third Friday in a row when they had not shown up.
As soon as I walked in I fell into a heap of sobbing on the *floor*. When
I had managed to collect myself
Go wash your face dear.
Pull yourself together.
Get to bed lie down and try to go to
I decided I would call. Before I called them I made certain that my
number was restricted from the view of anyone I called. I was not
calling them for talking.
Then what are you calling for? Don't call.
She answered. Never did she sound upset annoyed unnerved nor
angry or afraid. *Hello* she said again. She waited as if she were listening to an incantation being spoken. As if spell had finally delivered
speaker to a pause she said *Hello* again.
I was afflicted with a powerful sense of guilt when on that Friday
night I turned to see them seated in their usual corner spot. However
this new weighty burden also was invigorating to experience as if by
some strange art I had succeeded in delivering them to there myself.
I wondered if they knew the call had come from me. Because of how
she looked at me throughout the evening I determined that she knew.
I was convinced however that he did not know. Our little secret. On
that night we went to their estate. I was supposed to spend the night
but did not make it all the way. Still dark it was so very early in the
morning when they had me driven home. Next evening I stepped on
the platform looking down the line all doors all windows of the train.

Some people say that when they hear a person say that he or she had
no idea that something either was about to happen or it had been
going on for
for example criminal behavior
marital affairs
an unlocked little locked
My first night in that hotel when standing in the hallway listening
605
before I went back into my
I took the elevator down to 3. I walked. I did not see a thing on 3.
What does he look like I had asked.
You'll know him when you see him she had said.
Which room is yours I later asked her. Then
Which room is *his*.
These people say that people who insist that they had no idea about
such things are lying.
lacquered box.
I took the stairs to 4 then took the elevator up to 7 where the hallway
lights were out. Still nothing. No one. Took the stairs back down to 6.

I turned the corner entering a long transitional space that linked the statuary to the paintings in a gallery called *Baroque*. This long transitional space was covered on both sides with
mirror images
a matching painted reproduction of a set of draperies hanging from a fancy valance pulled together at each side with lavishly painted golden ropes that left me feeling weakened in the knees.
I did not go into *Baroque*.
Heart palpitations challenged by a draining queasiness throughout my limbs I claimed my things then started walking back as quickly as I could to that hotel.

Inside a KITCHEN doorway leading down into the BASEMENT (Night Six) she said *It's the oddest thing.* She said *I just don't see you very clearly in that big apartment building you are living in.* She said *I see the building in the distance. Getting closer I can see the walkway see the double doors can even see into a little of the lobby. I can feel your feelings hear your thoughts. Make out the numbers on your door.* She said *But I can't enter into where you live.*

She closed the BASEMENT off said *We won't go down there* then led me back upstairs.

The contrast was

The windows in the basement all have iron bars she said as we proceeded up. She said *And if I understand you half as well as I*

She stopped herself.

She turned looked back at me said *By the way do I detect in you a little*

Stopped.

The change in atmosphere as we proceeded from the STAIRCASE FROM THE KITCHEN TO THE BASEMENT to the STAIR-CASE HALL that led us back into the STUDY where he had been waiting for us with some special late night sweets produced in me immediate sensations of relief.

This was the night when I had been invited to stay the night but did not make it all the way.

cheeks pink eyes outlined blue blue lidded lashes body scented
blue no straps no cups legs shimmering sheerest blue shoes blue
blue velvet buckles ankle straps she waits inside this room in waning
candlelight where sapphire powder for her eyelids got into her eyes all
images dissolving in it as she lies down on the bed her face now floating down upon the blue tears staining streaks into the cotton white

I took the elevator up.

One day a man went out of doors to call out for his wife.

407

They gathered they petitioned on those walls that had been papered in the very same (607) aspects of an ordinary Chinese lifestyle. On the same red background brightly colored figures

As the man's wife had not answered any of his calls he had no option but to go into the forest searching.

argued to the judge

His heart beat rapidly as he imagined what he might discover in the forest and while he advanced he prayed that when he found his wife she would be safe. However at the same time he felt angry that his solitude had been disturbed.

But looking around I noted plenty of substantial differences as well. I put my tote bag on the *bed* unpacked a few things from my suitcase. For example just one nightstand. In addition to a one bulb ceiling fixture over the *bed* the pineapple lamp was small. Cream pleated shade. No floor lamps. No black table with a drawer below a shelf.

Although it was so early I turned down the very same leafy *bedspread* exposing the same pink

On the *bed* I laid my dinner long limp french fries hotdog mustard relish catsup packets on a towel.

The man recalled his house his chair and ottoman the gentle breezes through the open windows. So as not to lose his way he kept his path as straight as he could keep it. But what he had not anticipated when he went that afternoon into the forest was the movement of the outer and the inner rings of trees. Like gears rotating in opposite directions they were turning.

It's a little difficult to talk about she might have answered had he asked her whom she had been listening to that night when I had called them on the telephone. *But I will try. Each little story No let's say each song* she might have said. *It has an atmosphere.*
It would have been a cooler night on the VERANDAH where the feeling would be private. Intimate. Exclusive.
Something scampered up the screen.
This singer is in harmony with certain states of inner life she might continue *tuned into the same dimension as the song. What happens in a case like this is simply the inevitable effect of*
Do you see she might have said in an attempt to redirect
Each one is written on a plane.
I see he might have said. *A plane.*
Or if you like she might have said
one last attempt to put it in a form that he could understand
it floats within a world to which I momentarily attune as soon as I pick up the phone.

At other times he found himself transported back into the cloakroom where that woman who was much too old for such exhausting forms of labor would be cleaning organizing toilets hanging clothing on the racks. Down on her knees at first then standing stretching reaching in as far as she could reach
she'd even disappear in there
knees creaking
momentarily
then out again
still searching. He would watch her desperately flickering hands whose skeletal fingers rummaged hastily within the racks as seen from his perspective from that corner of the ceiling.
What's she looking for in there?
One day
It was a wretched day.
he turned into the park then chose a narrow pathway passing under trees with icy steely colored branches decorated with the white lights of the season. He stopped walking looked across the cracks upon the frozen lake but he was right away transported back to where the wheezing woman in the lower rack of clothing searching
reaching
going in
For what?
That was the time when she did come back.

I'll look for him
I told myself
a little later on.

Day 4

Next morning figuring good idea to go back where I'd started I was
in the reading room again. Grand hall watched over by elaborately
framed dark portraits shining facelessly from where they hung upon
the walls. Illuminated by the ceiling lights was dust from far too many
solitary arid paths picked up then carried in by lonely people who
had somehow made it to that place that seemed consumed by feelings
of true heartbreak
although entering into there was to attempt to lose oneself in notions
of imaginary heartbreak.
While the guidebook raved at its collection much of which could be
requested quickly fetched what left a more immediate impression was
the smell of alcohol enhanced with body odor. Wanting to look at the
people responsible for the smell competed in me with not wanting to
look at anyone who might look back. Also snaking its way in between
these divided desires was an irrational but profound physical impulse
to look at the smell itself.
It was a place that sat about in rags an edifice that looked out at the
world with such a weightiness a gloominess that truly was dismaying.

All those loiterers. Staff workers. Authors. Characters in the books. They all had lost resistance. On that day in fact it seemed as though the whole thing

books as well

had just passed out.

Having situated myself at the end of one of the reading tables I decided that I would go back to the hotel as early as possible check in eat dinner early go out look for him. Unless

I told myself

the seat adjacent to my seat now filling in

Unless I get to bed get up then catch the first train home show up tomorrow night for work. The question is I told myself how do I kill this afternoon.

It happened

as she told it

three months prior to the day when he was born.

Not me he reassured me winking leading us out to the VERANDAH.
(Night Two.) *Him* he said. He was so giddy as compared to her right
now. The difference: night to day. He pointed to a padded chair said
Please. She said *Sit down.* He said *I'll get the glasses.*

In her story it was morning when a gentleman first knocked upon
the door. Then late that night a figure showed up at her bed. The
gentleman in the doorway was deformed. The figure at the bed was
feminine though in describing this mysterious figure she did not say
female. She did not say *woman.*

With one match she lit the cluster of short candles in the center of the
table while he hurried to get the bottle open. *I had understood it that
the figure was an apparition* she said seating herself across from me.
He said *I can't remember* sitting down beside her. *Was it someone in
the family? Someone that we knew?*

A sadness sifted like pale sands behind her eyes as she replied that it
was neither friend nor family. She said *But the love that I was sensing
from this presence made me feel as though it had to be connected to me.*
Cheers he said. *Good friends.*

The presence told her

as she told us

pulling up her feet into the padded chair

She gave her nose a little blow.

that he

The being called him *he.*

would manage to accomplish something meaningful in life.

The point in telling us the story now as she explained was that the
meaningful had lately with the onset of these calls begun to signify
or possibly even point the way to something else. She told us that the
figure who had appeared at the end of her bed had always made her fear

For him she said.

this fear increasing with the coming up of certain birthdays. *How I dreaded all those numbers* she said returning to the other portion of the story

the deformed gentleman at the door. He knocked.

I asked what time.

What time? she said.

She didn't answer it.

But that was what the approaches of those birthday milestones did to me she said then going on to explain that through the years her focus had remained exclusively upon the figure who had appeared at the end of her bed. Hearing this

along with the further breakdown as to years months days

I started to imagine her surrounded by the glowing script of sleeplessness. Four date scrawled ghostly walls. A ceiling overnumbered doodled into spaces filling in around her night by night with ritualized yet ever frightening projected computations.

She said *But now I'm thinking about that ugly ugly*

In her face I saw his image taking shape.

In days that followed it
(THE NIGHT WE MET
FIRST FRIDAY NIGHT
NIGHT ONE which could have led to OVERNIGHT ONE
FIRST OVERNIGHT
continuing into
SATURDAY MORNING ONE
FIRST SATURDAY MORNING
MORNINGAFTER ONE
DAY TWO extending into NIGHT TWO
OVERNIGHT TWO
FIRST SATURDAY NIGHT which could
or more significantly
SUNDAY MORNING ONE
FIRST SUNDAY MORNING
MORNINGAFTER ONE
TWO
No. Get back. Look at the END OF THE WEEKEND ONE.
He said *The reason that he chose to carve the flowers into the façade
had little to do with decoration.*
Well at first it did she interrupted.
Yes he said. *At first. Quite right. But*
Shall we have our brandy now? she interrupted.
He got up advancing toward the cart that held the brandy things but
then continued to explain that there was something sinister that he
MB she interrupted.
Yes. MB. Of course she knows I'm talking about MB he said.
was something sinister that he was planning for the next inhabitants
of the manor whom he did not want to sell it to. He said *He had no
choice.* He said *He had to sell.* He said *As halfway through the building
process he lost all his*
NIGHT ONE.

NIGHT WE MET which should have led to
millions.
THE BEGINNING OF THE REST OF
Just imagine that she said.
Yes just imagine that he said.
but did not lead to that at all)
I often would experience a kind of achy feeling in my limbs as though
I'd taken a tumble.

On those days my eyes as if engaging in a nearly constant effort to
adjust from darkness often ached a little too. I felt a residue accruing
on my skin. More frequently I washed my hands my face I even took
an extra shower after work. One night just TWO NIGHTS AFTER
WE FIRST MET my shift beginning I was lighting the candles
on the little tables. On that night which could have been FIRST
SUNDAY
END OF WEEKEND ONE
but wasn't
I discovered that a previously somewhat meditative workplace ritual
now left me feeling desolate inside. Cleared out. Abandoned.
Looking down regretfully at a blackened fingertip I stood behind the
curtain that concealed supplies employee toilet that week's schedule
cartoon clippings pushpinned to the wall. I watched the patrons enter
through the open door across the lounge all smoking glowing like a
crowd of ghosts that simply could not wait to get inside.
Far more distressing though was what would happen on the nights
when I had laid my freshly shampooed head upon my pillow. Sleep
uninterrupted would arrive however entering into sleep I'd hear
a sound. I right away interpreted this sound as having traveled up
the elevator shaft to squeeze between the elevator doors turn left
accelerating down the hall another left another hall to drop down to
the space beneath my door. This sound as I was somehow made to
know originated as a whisper under my apartment building. Such an
up down corner whipping voyage rushing underneath my door had
been responsible for the whisper's gradual amplification of itself into
a voice.

I'll buy a post card
write a sentence
indicating that I
mail it
go home
never see them
speak to them again

I never spoke to them again.

I left the Public Library behind to return to the City Museum where
hungry after a somewhat forced examination of the items in the cases
arranged down the center of the long adjoining halls of *Ancient India*
I went for late lunch in the courtyard followed by an educational
(Headphones: Y) slow exploration of *Baroque*. As on the previous
day I felt so lonely in the crowd
handcuffed in fact
As if I had been strictly ordered not to meddle in that local war my
time within *Baroque* was not in line with outward objects conversa-
tions or activities.
Don't look.
Don't let yourself be seen.
yet there were instances when I was sure that I was being followed.
After a sudden departure from the room in which a famous series of
enormous allegories covered the walls I slyly disappeared into *Con-
temporary* then from there I quickly slipped into a small performance
space where a movie was showing to a room of empty seats.

Such interruptions to his waking life in which he found himself
transported back to
hovering
dangling
did not end when he grew out of
Passing for example through the outdoor winter market he might find
that he
No child
Not anymore
had been transported back into a corner of a floor to see that floating
yellowed now
the inset going brown the pearls among the tarnished bugle beads
comprising one long panel of decaying
lady

You see on THE NIGHT WE MET I also met a man who asked if he could take me home.

On one of these occasions she the lady slowly exited her dim boudoir in time for him to skitter past her into where at the conclusion of a journey partway up the doorframe he was gazing half in sorrow half in rage across the dismally deteriorated room.

The grape leaves then appearing at their edges to be curling

fruit appearing to have shifted slightly

bottom of a peach gone flat

there even was a little bruising in that precious painting given to the lady by his mother on that fateful night when

In the open cutting of the pomegranate he could see among the myriad shades of red the introduction

like a wicked presence in the paint

of black. It was as if within a scene in which it previously had been impossible to read the time of day that very day had now grown dim the futures of those fruits no longer guaranteed. Composed against a background clouded as if to suggest eternity

that carefully arranged array of angles shapes all guided by the level of the table top which now appeared to lean a little on the left

The basket. Look what's happening to the

Wait!

What time was it?

had started showing cracks the cracks increasing at the edges where the canvas met its tattered frame.

That's how it's creeping into there.

He meant of course the evil in the air.

To get to that first time (Night Two) when in the DRAWING ROOM the invitation came to stay the night I did not do a thing to show that I could see it coming. I just waited. Then I answered yes. That night I found a satin nightgown in the wardrobe in my bedroom. Satin robe. Pink slippers. In this bedroom moonlight softly passing through the gauzy sheers in layers white with cantaloupe I felt so good I felt real happiness I felt as though I'd slipped into a dream. I listened. I relaxed. I started out awake but as I drifted into sleep my sleep uninterrupted on that night

I thought I felt a tongue between my legs but when I checked there wasn't any tongue between my legs.

I closed my eyes to see a floating figure in a placid sea of pink. Translucent figure. Veins illuminated. Blood as white as snow.

The following morning
MORNINGAFTER ONE
DAY THREE

I woke up with a feeling of foreboding. Although fleeting there were aspects of this feeling that were substantiated as my gaze began to settle on that room traditional in its style of furnishings walls papered in a floral pattern corals pinks a space just occupied not dominated by the simply carved four poster canopied antique bed. On top of satin sheets there was a coverlet of white awash in roses pink with tangerine a springtime pattern made to look alive by lime green satin thread embroidered into leaves appearing to have nestled permanently among the blooms. The carpeting a deeper shade of pink there were two nightstands each draped in a doily underneath a crystal lamp. A whisper thin ornately shaded floor lamp arched above a little country English chair rose velvet with a fuchsia cushion unexpected as an accent reminiscent though of matching objects in the sitting room as well as bathroom hand towels.

Drowsy.

Anxious.

Little bit uncertain about the protocol for such a morning I remained in bed where drifting into thoughts producing frosty images that melted at the corners I recalled the piece of land that we had stood upon where once a tiny house had been. As if in pictures blending into one another I saw trails of footprints made on floors that weren't there anymore. Above those trails I spied a row of body sized increasing in their size impressions left in beds except the beds were gone. Surrounding all of this were scatterings on top of scatterings of tiny imprints made from fingers up down missing windows missing from the walls that were not there.

I sat in back. Before those rows of empty seats there loomed upon the movie screen a shoeless little pigtailed girl in overalls whose face was never shown. She seemed to be the costar to the dark sophisticated man who wore a hat. That man was constantly together with the girl though both were strangers to each other. She apparently unsupervised he was alone as well inside an art museum where they both were looking at the drawings all too delicate to be discernable by us. In fact they shared that movie screen exclusively until a dark haired woman in dark glasses entered catalyzing the expansion of the picture to include a male security guard. Along with the idea of filming a movie meant to be projected in a gallery inside an art museum

inside an art museum

seeing as the essential *action* in the movie issued from the man's encounter with the woman

they

the other characters

both came across as far too obviously contrived. What the moviemaker did seem good at knowing though was how to cause the sexuality of the woman the desire of the man the blandness of the security guard to wipe their hands off

as it were

upon the little girl.

Awakened
standing up
she has her bearings now inside this pale blue room that seems to
have been situated on the line dividing one world from another. In
that other world there is a pretty little stream bright flowers springtime leaves. She sees the stream as clearly as if she were looking at it
through an open window. On the glassy surface of the water myriad
luminous beings
tiny little things
go gliding by.
Then suddenly the candle out the room's gone dark.

I sometimes feel as though I've known you since before we even met she told me. We were on a blanket by the river looking toward the compli-cated NORTH FACADE. He'd gone to get the picnic baskets. *Do you feel that way?*

(Day Six)

Within the angle of the L comprising the NORTH FAÇADE an elaborate sequence of roofs ran down the hill

She said *You may not know this but I*

spilling toward the river in three long descending divisions.

She looked back as if to check on where he was.

She closed her eyes took in a breath then said *I seize all chances when your mind is open to insert my thoughts straight into you.* She said *So I must beg you* be *a little patient with me please because I cannot always be as quick as you would like.*

The highest of these three divisions housed the STAIRCASE MAIN distinguished by large *Traceried* (Day One) *windows* he had said. *Which means there's stone around them.*

Scooting further toward the blanket's edge I tried increasing what small distance lay between us but she reached as if to take my hands in hers but then pulled back to say *Just think of it like this.*

She said *I'm working at my desk.*

She said *You know what I mean by* desk?

While water gathered in my mouth a moving image took possession of my mind a towering purple plume black curling lines on crisp white pages turning over in the wind. We saw him coming down the FIVE STONE STEPS. He had the picnic baskets. She spoke quickly *And I'm writing.* Softly. *You are at your desk.* Somewhat accusingly. *And you are writing too.*

When getting closer he called *Hungry anybody?*

Desperately she whispered *Tell me what you're writing!*

Headed back to the hotel that afternoon I took an unfamiliar side street linking up diagonally to a fashionable tree lined boulevard where I could not help stopping at a chic department store display of mannequins dressed left to right increasing in their level of formality. All three had hairless heads that were identical although with added glamour came more makeup on the faces of the heads.

Confused about the way from there to my hotel I turned disoriented

dizzy even

tired

I backtracked

tried but couldn't find it on the pullout map included with the guidebook so I

How could this be happening I asked myself.

At last en route as best as I could calculate I walked recalling eyes cheeks lips all features that for those who passed the window from the left would be remembered as a growingly provocative progression. That's not right I told myself.

Not merely anxious I was really nervous. It was getting late. I made it back to the department store

Thank God.

deciding I would go the way I came. Get back to the museum. Then from there it's travel the familiar course. Back to the drugstore. Market. Then

However this impression would be challenged rather violently as I had just discovered

by a story of emerging innocence: a gradual diminishment of lips cheeks eyes to be remembered by those having passed the window from the right.

It's delicate she said.

He said *Yes we will give you some advice on how to handle him*. He said *He's smart*.

She said *He's not just smart*. She said *It's more than that*. She looked me in the eye but spoke to him. *She'll know exactly how to handle him* she said.

The talk about the giving of advice (DAY THREE or SATURDAY ONE) ideally would have happened in the car when we were riding to the station or when we were stopped outside the station in the car. But this talk happened (MORNING TWO) down near the BOAT-HOUSE.

That night
NIGHT THREE
START OF WEEKEND ONE
we all went straight upstairs. Its entrance indicated by an antique lyre
backed chair my room was saturated. Colored. Patterned. Every surface
decorated. Walls red. Carpet red. The bedding an explosion of white
roses on the red. No sitting room although there was a fireplace whose
grate was painted black. The bathroom walls were papered silver. White
towels white carnation soaps white fluffy rug beside the tub all complemented with a little silver chair black cushion silver stars embroidered.
In the bedroom underneath a mirror framed in silver leaf there was an
ivory painted secretary with an ivory seat. When lights were out the
secretary glowed the seat glowed too as if they had been carved out of
the moon. Again there were no blinds beneath the gauzy curtains. We
were in the country. There was no one sneaking peeks at us out there.
When earlier on that night I stepped out of the car I felt I had exhil-
aration in my arms my legs as if my soul were suddenly expanding
under rays of noonday sun. We all went straight upstairs. I went to
sleep. However though my sleep it's true did pass uninterrupted I
awakened. Thus on MORNINGAFTER TWO or SATURDAY
MORNING TWO continuing into OVERNIGHT THREE or
NIGHT THREE into MORNINGAFTER THREE my day
began too early.
I pulled out a red silk robe red slippers. Went into the hallway. All was
silent. Dark. Apparently the only one awake I crept around the corner
past the little antique bookcase then continuing down the hall until I
came up to the door into the NURSERY
DAY. I did not try the door. However when I stopped before that
door I suddenly recalled with some confusion that the last time I
I felt a chill beneath my skin.
How are you ever going to stand the pain of it when all of this is gone?
The countless days
The endless nights

I made it back to the hotel that evening only to discover there was nothing left.

Excuse me but is that thing working right I said into the tiny hole in the reception window. It says nothing's left.

According to the form behind the frosted window there were vacancies on 2. There also were some vacancies on

3

4

5

Apparently a number's being dark

6

7

did not mean the room was taken. Even 8. The way it worked was if the credit card transaction went through spitting out the key into the tray then you could rest assured except for rarest instances the room had been available.

So he the person I'll be looking for he is he is your son then I had asked her. At this moment we were on the VERANDAH having recently returned from the CORNER

SOUTHMOST of the estate where a tiny house once stood.

He's not our son she said.

I took the elevator up to 5 ascending through a building that seemed empty from the bottom to the top.

He's not?

That morning
after struggling some
Hey sleepyhead. A gentle knocking on my door.
Whose there.
She said *You hungry?*
I awakened with a sense that while I slept I had received a long trans-
mission during which my inner self had been awake. I understood
that this communication met me as vibrations coming from a group of
beings who were sometimes small at other times enormous. Irrespec-
tive of their sizes I recalled these creatures as
collectively
a dazzling play of light in everchanging forms.
I'll be right down I answered after which I felt anticipation of a devastating sense of deprivation from which I was sure that once it started I
would not be able to recover.

503
Headboard
Arcing row of tulips painted pastel colors.
Curtains white.
The underblind white vinyl.
I pulled down the underblind as soon as I walked in the door.
There were no pictures on the *walls* just squares of patterned *fabric*
under glass that needed to be cleaned.
The *bed* was covered in a navy *bedspread. Bed* was framed in lathe
turned posts all painted white
all scratched of course
two nightstands
scratched
a little oval table
scratched
The *carpeting*

As she explained

the last time they had seen him was at home.

And I remembered telling myself she said *that there was something quite significant about what I had witnessed.*

It was cool on the VERANDAH. (Night Five.) Seeing as a smallish walking tour had passed through roped off portions of the mansion during the day the feeling now was intimate. Entrancing. She explained that this

the last time she had seen him

was at nighttime. Hearing something

Had a funny feeling she said.

she had gotten out of bed gone downstairs to the kitchen seen him leaving through the kitchen door. She said *And after that I went into the sitting room. Just waited.*

We were enjoying dinner on the VERANDAH after having spent the afternoon down by the BOATHOUSE so as to avoid the guests when they were passing through the mansion with their guide.

She said *But trying now to figure out what was significant about that sighting would*

Require fabrication on her part he interrupted.

That is what he always says she said. *What do you think?*

was
navy
too
with
speckles
woven
in
the
navy
that
were
white
not
hungry
gnawing
stomach
so
I
lowered
my
uneaten
dinner
down
into
the

He said *I'll be back.*

She said *Me too. We'll be right back.*

Within the interval of their absence I became aware of something troubling in the atmosphere that permeated not just the VERANDAH but the whole of the estate. I also felt it all around the car two evenings later when I got into their car when they showed up to take me to the train.

Unlike the other nights on which I
402
had been awakened
407
by those cries that I could neither locate nor identify
On this night
503
the sound was more like singing
faintness having been the likely explanation for its failure to awaken me
from dreaming. In the dream I slept inside a room that as I understood
was mine. I heard the softest sound a singing barely more than whis-
pers. In its failure fully to awaken me it caused in me a kind of split.
The room in which I slept was perfumed with the scent of roses.
When I heard this voice that only partially had awakened me
the waking part of me
as if it had been touched in ways the sleeping part could never have
been touched
then lifted out of me. It was an airy being peeling layer off of layer
from my sleeping body in the bed. This being's lifting off of me had
caused my eyes to open. Watching from the bed I saw it hover then
advance until it stopped. It then began to right itself into a pose like
someone standing
feet remaining off the ground
then floated toward the door which opened as it neared it. From the
bed I tracked its floating out the door into a darkness that I understood
as dangerous but there was nothing I could do. The being's sleeping
dress was just like mine in back. It had my hair. My body's shape. I
tried to call to it. I even tried to get up out of bed go after it. No use. It
disappeared into the dark. What's more I had already drifted back to
sleep. My point of view then transferred from the body in the bed
from me
to her

into the body that had floated out the door. So watching from my brand new floating self I looked back quickly checking taking note of 503

before emerging down the hall of darkness leading into still more halls of darkness. One by one they pulled me through them tilting me then sliding rocking sinking me as if I went through water. That the voice did not get louder softer meant that I was never getting closer to it farther from it.

Suddenly I saw a tiny window lit up in the distance. Black lines crisscrossed on the window which was round. The window was

as I could understand with zero doubt as I was sinking closer to that crisscrossed iron pattern window

where the voice the singer was. Indeed as I approached I saw that there was someone in there backlit looking out at me.

But when I looked out from behind that window I forgot about the singer.

I

my point of view that is

You see my point of view had transferred to the pair of eyes behind the window instantly it seemed.

Through those dark eyes I looked out through the bars

for me

for her

There was nobody there.

THE NIGHT WE MET I also met a man whose question about a ride I answered in accordance with my policies on rides.

Awakened suddenly I got out of the bed put on my coat my boots my stomach digging at me no snacks left no interest. I went out into the hallway took the elevator all the way to 8 where down the hall wedged open was a door that led me to another staircase leading to the roof. I'm getting out of this I told myself as I emerged onto the roof. Tomorrow I am going home.

He stops looks up from where he stands but suddenly his vision is
obscured not by the raking sun but by a kind of glaze that coats his
eyes. He turns back heads in the direction of the park where he will
hesitatingly
You should not go in there. You have a job to do.
proceed in the direction of the shimmering autumn colors lake.

Day 5

Next morning after breakfast I walked through the playground then the park returned to the hotel to pick up all my things to drop the key into the slot head for the station catch the first train home get back in time for work. However as if acting in accordance with the orders of an unknown mechanism operating from an unidentifiable location I betrayed my plan by opening up the guidebook after exiting the patio then taking turns resulting in my after quite a hike arrival at the waterfront. From there I took the (Transportation: Ferry) to the Summer Castle nearly hidden behind apparently impenetrable hedges. This one was the most romantic most enchanting underappreciated as the guidebook put it (Peak: Spring/Summer) of the (Recommended: Y).

From where he stands outside the gate the park appears to have transformed itself into a broad arcade of mirrored corridors that lead to spaces that have been closed off. The glaze upon his eyes distorts his vision. Marble columns
terra cotta columns
plaster
seem pulled out of their alignment
propped up. Smells of autumn leaves. The smoke from nearby chimneys.
Longing for a rest he walks until he finds the benches that surround the lake.
The park seems recently to have been rearranged along two overlapping axes that produce a pair of vistas. Space that once flowed freely into space now seems to have been cut up walled off into regions into which no one can pass. *Is someone sitting next to me?* He looks then looks behind him slantwise peering back at rows of glowing gray divisions separating corridor from corridor discerning statues that are still from statues moving under coverings he knows as treetops. All of this reflected in tall mirrors framed by spaces in between the columns. From these figures he hears laughing. Talking. Squinting he would swear that he can even hear some kissing. Generally speaking this whole place expresses attitudes of mind that are unfeeling unconcerned entirely ignorant of his suffering. Turning again
Real suffering.
he looks across the lake.
Unlike the park itself which seems to have been cut up separated into parts the lake has spilled into a wide expanse of brokenness. He sees it as a lake of heavy gilt framed mirrors laid down side by side as if across a surface that the undergrowth combined with what's pushed up from down below has made uneven all the varying angles of reflection having come together in a glittering array of shattered light.
Like splendid papers hung on walls that hold framed portraits of imposing faces

Like deep patterned rugs laid down beneath the finest carved scrolled wooden feet
Like heavily embellished curtains drawn across broad windows
looking out on what was grown there dug up out of there dragged off from there
I'd swear that there is someone sitting next to me right now.
we are reminded
No there's no one sitting next to you.
Where did she go?
to look at something else.
Get out of here. Go get her.

Who?

Arriving at the castle on the main path from the south
proceeding around the corner to the moated gateway on the north
then through this gateway to the inner wall
through NORTH GATE into STABLE
past the east or KITCHEN front
through two more big gates down below
depositing me at last onto the SOUTH FACADE
I circled it
my rolling suitcase struggling on these old time surfaces
without apparent end in view but with a feeling of pure joy
enlightenment
deep drawn awareness of the beauty in the tragedies on top of tragedies
that I perceived in this location gotten to by boat. As I grew conscious
of such feelings my entire being filled up with desire. This new sensation touched me so profoundly that I wished to get as close as I
In other words I hoped I prayed to find a way to pull it deep enough
into myself that I
I mean I wanted just to take that castle
lie down naked on those ruined grounds
my legs spread open
shove that castle straight up into me.

He has resumed his course. He turns a corner moving along as if this journey had been permanently coded into him by someone something
situated on the other side of somewhere else. While there are times when suddenly he finds himself in places where the agony of being sent to there is more than he can
There are many other times when he is totally unable to abandon present circumstances. At those times he begs to be transported back.

When leading us up the FIVE STONE STEPS he said *It's just so lucky that we met.*
It's nothing to do with luck she said.
Atop of the FIVE STONE STEPS we hooked around the COR-NER
NORTHWEST of the mansion. Picturesque bay windowed spot for peering into the DRAWING ROOM.
I thought I saw a form behind the glass. He took me by the arm. He turned us all around.

THAT NIGHT
NEXT NIGHT
when I got up walked out into the hall I found that I was standing at
the door into the NURSERY
DAY. I did not try the door. I turned. I took the STAIRCASE
MAIN
down to the ENTRANCE
MAIN. I then went back up to my room.

No. That's not true. I went into the
Fourth door on the left.
to see the little lacquered box beside the oval mirror on the mantel
underneath the
photographic painting of a house.

Now looking through the windows she can see a figure moving down below contorted trees above the twisted roots that cover everything. She pulls the curtains closed. She lies down on the bed looks all around her at the floor.

Thus with the sighting of a movement that cannot be stopped has come anticipation of a cover of patina creeping over every surface like a shoreline onto which a rolling tide encroaches.

The interior of that castle
as the little pamphlet indicated
had at one time been an antiquarian chiaroscuro. Open framework
open timber roofs elaborate chimneypieces in the hall with other
lesser chimneypieces in the rooms. So many painted decorations.
Finest frescoes on the walls adorned with armor
weapons
heraldry
high stained glass windows
plaster busts
Etruscan vases
pictures
tapestries
The castle
it was written
had been built up through the years
a tower added here
there
blasted
some things taken away
put back
torn down
Too tired to fight it anymore that castle obviously had gone behind
the hedge allowed itself to be completely opened up then shot up into
turned all inside out.

THAT NIGHT
NIGHT FIVE
I went down to the KITCHEN opened up the corner door then
started down the stairs into the BASEMENT.

On the train awakened by another even bigger jolt
amazingly
I managed slipping back into that dream again.
Clock ticking on the wall inside the cottage I fell sound asleep.
WITHIN THE DREAM INSIDE THE COUNTRY COT-
TAGE DREAM I then was given information
somehow
that the dying of the little boy was nothing but a big mistake.
The little boy
as I was made to know
was meant to be alive.
I woke up from THE DREAM WITHIN THE
clock not ticking
COUNTRY COTTAGE DREAM
still in the OUTER COTTAGE DREAM
elated
dropping tears of joy
true happiness
immeasurable relief. I hurried over to the bedroom door which was
completely covered up with vines with tiny blooms. I opened it.
My job WITHIN THE COUNTRY COTTAGE DREAM was
Take that information about the life into the bedroom. Take it to the bed
that has the tiny body of the boy on top of it. Then shake the body tell the
boy that he was meant to be alive.
However there was not a body in the bed.
Just shake the boy!
clock ticking again

When I got back on board the ferry
leaving behind the honey colored stony clusters of the fallen gables
crumpled towers
toppled
candy wrappers
walls
no longer high
dilapidated
broken bottles
heaps of rock
surrounded by the weakened but remarkably undestroyed stone
battlements encircled by a moat
tin cans
I thought about my feelings as with all of my belongings with me I
had walked the pamphlet in my hand around that castle.
I was not its only visitor although I might as well have been. The cool
fall air that heralded the onset of the winter winds intensified the
feeling of desertion. Isolation.
Crushed.
Save pigeons
seagulls shrieking
wheeling endlessly through ruined walls
the moat long since closed in with tall weeds thick reeds grasses
rippling over what according to the pamphlet had at one time been
the widest smoothest lawns
was anything but inviting. Watching from the ferry little could be seen
except a wall of overgrowth
the garden wall was smothered by the saplings.
towers soaring
plunging
Though it was apparently inanimate I feared that I had managed to
awaken it that day igniting a continuation of the terribly steady stalled

slow process of its creeping crawl upon the surface of the earth. It
carried all its emptiness
its endless infestations
with it.
As the ferry pulled away I half expected I would see that castle
coming after me.

What do you think you're doing coming all the way down here? she said.

Next morning

Which one?

Doesn't matter. There would be no others after that.

That night I took the elevator up.

THE NIGHT WE MET
THE NIGHT I ALSO MET A MAN who asked if he could drive
me home
if I had answered otherwise I might have ridden IN ANOTHER
CAR out to another mansion facing an enormous courtyard orga-
nized around a flame. Upon a balcony above a central entrance might
have hung a bell. *That bell will ring*
as he
my new companion
might have told me with his hand so gently at my back
whenever we want to celebrate. Above the entrance left of center might
have stood a bronze winged female figure arm extended toward a
garden on the other side of which there might have stood a little
gallery containing
Souvenirs.
as my companion would have said.
Mementos.
Various outdoor sections of the grounds would link by patios connecting by vine covered archways to a networked garden whose main
artery
a hall of blooming flowers
would have led INTO A HOTHOUSE.
IN THE MANSION HIGH ABOVE THE STAIRWAY
seen upon first entering it
there might have hung the mural of all murals.
Just to see it there
together
my companion
I
to see them all up there
a panorama into which his image
my companion's

You will too my precious. Someday.
would be added
might make my companion very sad escorting me through the spacious rooms devoted to
The greatest most enduring name in all these lands.
Their crest would show on crystal vases furniture in paintings porcelain dishes silver serving pieces china
No there are no casual encounters he would later whisper as we walked
INTO THE HOTHOUSE where exotic blooming sweet intoxication had awaited us.
At times
although I would not want to let him go
because of my companion's deep felt sadness for his many loved ones
lost
including
someday
me
I'd wish for nothing more than I would wish for his immediate departure from this earth.

702

The paper on the *walls* a dingy peeling floral pattern was at one time surely very happy looking against crown molding that had once been white but now was not. Above the *fireplace* there was a mirror hanging opposite another mirror neither of them new. The windows had lace *curtains* on them. Underblinds on both. Upon the dresser there were two brass candlesticks. No candles. On a little table near the door there was a shiny Chinese serving tray that looked as if it had been brought in there then left there. On the *bed* there was a simple yellow *bedspread*.

I put down my things then laid a towel across the *bed*.

I started to unpack but then I stopped.

I put the serving tray upon the towel took out my dinner from the sack looked over at the *wall*.

THAT NIGHT
THE NIGHT I TOLD HIM NO
If I had told him yes I might have found a way to get

What do you think of all of this he asked me. She had gone to check on dinner. It was chilly out there in the moonlight on a pathway hugging the periphery of the mansion where he had been taking me on a stroll. He pointed out the KITCHEN then adjacent to its outdoor EN-TRANCE

KITCHEN

was the SCULLERY

outdoor entrance: none

Then turning there we passed the ENTRANCE

SERVANTS'

followed by the DINING ROOM

no outdoor entrance

followed by

still talking

so much telling

asking

surreptitiously

no touching yet

not yet

the ENTRANCE

NORTH

MAIN

which contained the secret

On my neck there was I thought just for a moment heavy breathing. entrance to the STUDY. Then we turned the corner on the DRAW-ING ROOM'S no entrance skirting around to the VERANDAH

outside entrance

No of course there was no outside way of getting into the VERANDAH.

after which we passed the STUDY

followed by two darkened rooms

dark windows

then the outside of an even darker room he called THE PRIVATE
ROOM.
We stopped.
He stared straight through my coat my shirt my bra.
They all had bars. The basement windows. They although so low
were visible on all faces of the mansion.
So it's under everything I told myself as we reversed our course then
headed for the ENTRANCE
MAIN our having seen her through the windows. As if naked I began
to tremble. She was in the STUDY looking out.

WITHIN THE DREAM IN WHICH I LOOKED DOWN AT
THE BED IN WHICH THE LITTLE BOY IT HAD BEEN
LEARNED WAS MEANT TO BE ALIVE I cried.
I walked back through the vine entangled doorway in the cottage
stepping on the scattering of little flowers
dropping tears onto the floor
those flowers
pieces of a broken plate
Of course the body wasn't there. I had observed the body's vanishing
on the plate. Of course the fucking body wasn't there.

He takes the elevator up.

702

Right after eating my spaghetti I began to peel that floral paper back.

The following morning we were in the DRAWING ROOM. She said *And it was such a large and leafy plant it wasn't anything that any of the children in my neighborhood had ever seen.*
It was a story whose beginnings somehow had skipped over me. I felt distracted. Frightened even. Strange.
He said *It had a giant jelly blob of orange right in the center of it.*
She said *And I was among a group of children standing around the plant and I*
Around the big orange blob you mean he interrupted.
She said *And I felt upon that day what I will now refer to as Exquisite nausea* he interrupted.
No she said. *Exquisite*
He poured
coffee in our cups as she described this feeling as a feeling that can serve as someone's introduction to the act of linking that occurs *That must occur* she said *because one cannot bear the picture that is current.* She said *And that linking into other pictures will continue for as long as we*

The man who went into the woods to find his wife no longer thought about his wife. He thought of nothing other than the movements of the forest rings that turned in opposite directions and at inconsistent speeds. As if so many days had passed the man felt empty as a person feels from fasting and it was within this period when deciding he could go no farther that the man sat down upon a stump. An animal appeared. It was a wolf that soon became a bear that then became an eagle. Through the transformations of the animal the man could feel a watchful presence all around him but he felt the presence most intensely when the eagle began to change

its wings retracting

petrifying head

first legs then body

leaving not a skeleton but just one bone that shot up from the ground into the air. As bone reached apex of its arc the sky took on the colors of a sunset. But before the bone's descent began

as if the forest's rings had synchronized

clicked into place

unlatched

an opening in the trees appeared.

The man then found that he was exiting onto a wide and sandy moonlit beach.

For when the body isn't there it doesn't matter if the life can be pre-served. It doesn't matter if it somehow was a big mistake about the death.

Then suddenly the man was once again engulfed by trees.

But if he isn't your son
I asked
who is he?

Softly

secretly

the door has closed behind him now that he has stepped into this room

the candle out

in which he somehow sees from every corner

angle.

All perspectives being his

he instantly

How did I get here?

She is lying on the bed.

Who is she?

Bit of moonlight's all there is. It casts a soft blue glow all over everything until his vision sharpens. Then

as if this story finally has delivered him

At last!

to where he has been headed from the start

he can devour her with his gaze.

He sees her in black velvet with tucked black tulle filling in the
bodice narrow straps run down the shoulders forming a V in back.
Her weeping can be noted in the quivering of the second shoulder
straps that form the armholes into which is set a crushed tulle sleeve
that falls just slightly over atop the arms. A heavy band of sequins
black with sumptuous jet beading thoroughly embellishes the bodice
back from which hang ropes of more jet beads. The loops as he can
see continue underneath the arms where they are caught up at the
neckline. To the underportion of the sleeve hang tassels

black

connecting to a black silk cording slung across the hipline. Wide
black sequined bands of beads

jet

link the neckline back down to the hip. A long black skirt extends into
a pointed train in back that hangs so gently off the bed.

The stark severity of the blackness of this gown is unrelieved with the exception of one band of iridescent sequins mixed with opalescent beads with sea pearls interlacing with the beading at the hipline. It is for that glittering glowing hipline that he reaches.

You know just exactly who he is she said.

I do?

DOOR ONE
DOOR TWO
were locked.
(It's wrong. I went down to the STUDY. But I did not go directly to
the STUDY.)

Wrong again. My sleep was not uninterrupted that first night. I did awaken. I went out into the hallway stopped before the door into the
NURSERY
DAY.
I tried the door. As I remember it
the door into the NURSERY
DAY was locked.

Next night I went down to the STUDY where I saw the little
lacquered box beneath the photographic painting of a house. Snow-
capped. Turned out it was a winter scene but flowers bloomed in
front. Up in the window
top right
I made out a figure
standing
with it looked as if a darker figure standing just behind it. But I couldn't
say for sure because the figures had already disappeared as soon as I had
Yes
No
But
That next
next
night
DOOR TWO
DOOR THREE
were locked.
But ONE
I don't know what possessed me to experiment with ONE.
was open.
What I saw in there was shocking although there is always something
troubling in observing people when they do not know
But did they know? They had to know.
that you are watching them. To witness such a scene from back
behind a hole bored in a wall is one thing but to see it from a slightly
open door is something else. Those two in long dark robes were in
the middle of the carpet crouching over something. Though they did
not make a motion to acknowledge me I felt as if they wanted me to
see them so engaged. But what enhanced the shocking nature of this
sighting was the spot upon the carpet which I clearly saw when they
rose up abandoning that room to enter the adjoining room.

Nobody in there anymore
ROOM ONE
I slowly entered from the hallway into
Furniture draped. ROOM ONE. The pictures draped. That room
all dark except for light collecting at a candle in the window. Smells of
dust with molded over mustiness the room had obviously been shut
off. Sealed up. *So well preserved* he might have said. There quivering
in the candle's radiance the spot upon the carpet was a narrow one.
From something spilling no doubt from a person moving toward the
window from the door. Unless it had been window
door. As if it had been treated with a time released solution of remov-
ers it just disappeared as I was looking down at it.

702

Beneath the floral paper was a different floral paper.

So I entered the adjacent room by passing through the left ajar
interior door as they had done. But they weren't there. When I looked
over at the other door the door out to the
DOOR TWO
Second on the
hallway
I could see that it was open. So I exited that room looked in the hallway saw that there was no one in the hallway went back in the room.
ROOM TWO
Still darker than the first room
curtains drawn
the only light was light that came in from the room
ROOM ONE
that had the candle in it.
In this darker more unkindly room there was the feeling that there
were so many little creatures crawling on the borders creepies hung
up in the corners dropping
legs up
on the carpet.
Through an open door connecting this room to the next room I went
in the next room just as
I had gathered
they had done.

Then peeling that one back revealed another one.

It was a room that made me feel like lying down as if to walk into the sticky cobwebbed feeling of it was to get a quick transfusion from the veins of someone sleeping soundlessly for seven hundred years. It was at first completely dark.

My robe came off.

She's cheap.

I heard the whispering.

She's desperate.

She's unseemly.

In this room I felt them walking toward me felt them kissing me all over.

Dirty girl!

They led me to the center of the room then lowered me to a carpet that I felt so ready for. I heard their robes fall off. They then began to offer themselves to me

a mouth

a breast

She whimpered.

Someone had a mole.

unless

unless

I felt an insect somewhere on me.

more slow licks

light quick vibrations

came between my legs. He got on top of me. Then she. Beginning here I saw an atmosphere within the darkness start to glow as if it were illuminated by the borrowed light that burned within their bodies leaking through their eyes that shone like balls thrown in the air above me kept aloft by so much heavy breathing. Panting. Moans were helpful in identifying who was who but truly there was no detective work to do in there.

His

Hers

Hands
Bodies
Voices
They played out a scene of jealousy
me in the middle
Fucking me so slowly he allowed her
Sad vibrations came to me delivered from the soul of her in through
the skin of me. I thought I felt a mouse run by when he objected to
her crying into both my hands that she had somehow taken into her
possession. Then he redirected. Let her have them. Likewise after all
his begging pleading suddenly she acquiesced permitting him to be all
over me as he then granted that her breasts could come down onto me
my mouth
before he kissed me
He broke in again
she moaning into me
he sending all his semen racing up down all the empty halls of me

Who do you think you are?

Another layer under that.

The next night I went down directly to the STUDY where I saw the little lacquered box beside the oval mirror on the mantel underneath the photographic painting of a house.

More to the point she said to me *whatever made you think that you could come down here and open this?*

I didn't open it I said.

This was the night when I was meant to stay the night. The night when I had asked her at the start of it which room was his.

Which one I asked again.

It was a question that she neither answered nor acknowledged asking me instead why didn't I take a seat why didn't I have a piece of maple praline cake.

But now

But this

They had me driven home by taxicab. Next evening I looked down the line. The sky already growing dark. The platform even darker. Cutting through the coming night a row of lighted windows of a train. When I arrived at this hotel I stepped into the patio. I told myself He's here.

Then under that next layer was

I'll try again.

When I arrived on that first night I took the elevator down to 3 then took the stairs to 4 the elevator up to 7 where the hallway lights were out. But I was wrong about that night.

That night I saw a man.

Perhaps it was the time of night perhaps my own fatigue that colored my impression of this man who walked

He moved as if

The glimpse of walking I had witnessed told me that

with arms held stiffly to his sides as though were they to be released his hands would have begun to scrabble frantically along the walls.

Back down to 6

I was approaching 605 when I

There's something going on in there I told myself.

When he was passing by I

All but certain of his turning looking back at me I did not turn look back at him. I hurried back into just paint.

The walkway she said
double doors
your feelings even
thoughts.
She said *But I can't enter into where you live. Sometime you'll have to*
tell me what it's like.

It's green.

It's green?

Uh huh.

But it's a green of varying gradations like a forest full of trees.

I took the elevator up to 8.

(Night Six) She closed the BASEMENT off.

When I am out of it I get back into it by walking. But before I walk
I have to work. When work is done I blow the little candles on the
tables out. I get my tote bag from behind the curtain. Out the door. I
walk. Between my legs I feel a sadness. Loneliness. I think: When I
am home again engulfed I'll drop down to my knees upon the floor
where I will pray to *bed* to *floors* to *windows* even to my *walls* to be
delivered from all this. But I can't get to there. Not yet. I have to walk.
Before I walk I have to work.

I light the little candles on the tables work all corners of the room until the time has come to blow the candles out. I get my tote bag from
behind the curtain. Out the door. I do not take a taxicab. I walk. I hear
that voice*: Instead of looking wanton try to give the sense that you are
dressed in a diaphanous material.*

You wear a wreath of flowers on your hair.

It's true your body seems to have been made for pushing to the earth.
For doing ugly business to.

But try.

*Impart instead the information that if hands approach you will
collapse into an aura that will take the form of mist.*

I get up off the floor. I wash my face. I pull myself together. Get into
my bed reflecting on the night.

I tell myself: Tonight you worked all corners of that room. You blew
those candles out. You went behind that curtain peed then got your
things together. Out the door. You walked right by those taxicabs.
The bus stop. Felt the crying slipping out of you. It dribbled down
your legs. You walked it off. You looked. Fuck you. Fuck all of you.
You shook it off. You let them look. You tried conveying the impression that you

softly

two angelic sleeves

each fastened at the cuff

with pearls

three tiny brooches
at the shoulder
nosegay at the waist
a pair of silver sandals
iridescent
ribbons
tied around your ankles

Wrists as well?

You see.

I work.

I walk.

I look the bodies up down. Mainly look at men. Among the men if I looked only at the ones that seemed most plastic I would not find any man. Therefore I look at every man. If he looks back at me too rigidly I look beyond him. I accelerate. I get away. When I am fixed on one who seems as plastic as I like a man to seem I speak to him. I say as I have heard it said so many times before: *Come home with me feel wrapped in all my sympathy. For sympathy defines my being. It is everything in me.*

I see a man. The man sees me. The man looks adequately plastic so I don't accelerate. Don't try to get away. He walks with me. He talks. This man. I talk to him. I say: There are not many people who are capable of accepting the idea of multiple existences on earth. Do you know what I'm saying to you sir?

He answers *Such discussions will not get us anywhere* as we approach the walkway leading to the double doors of my apartment building.

He says *For too many of us life can only be a simple episode*

We take the elevator to my floor.

a fragment not a whole in which all feelings of belonging must be lost forever.

Up on 8 the little door up to the roof was still propped open.

This
I tell the man
is where I live.

Black rubber roofing underfoot the view of iron fire escapes on build-
ings building tops high walls of windows most of which were dark
was backdropped by a starry sky. I saw some movement in a window
just across from
It was there
when looking out from there where I began to
For perhaps as people say the first time in my life I felt as if
*There comes a time when one has to become completely conscious of all
joys as well as every kind of suffering on this earth.*
That window. A suggestion of a form behind it.
All of my determination rooted in sincerest confidence that I could
find him here that I could bring him back to her
To us he said.
were leveled.
There is someone in there looking back at me I told myself.
It was not only the suggestion of a form in shadows in that other
building's window but it also was a face that in its image lay the image
of itself depicted as if from all possible points of view.
This sighting of a man or woman hard to tell was followed by the
onset of deep longing.
Man.
A comprehensive loneliness.
Demolished.
Right away I told him she's the one she said.
That's what she said to me he said. *She told me that you were the only one.*
I didn't open it I said. I didn't even try to open it I said.
But when I said it to her I could only hear could only see
recall
as if this image had been overlaid on top of everything
the tiny body of a bird inside that lacquered box
Man.
bird

To touch its tiny body was to rub an opening in the body that
revealed it was a body full of tiny ants
all black
all dead
packed in.

But how could flowers
carved ones
ones in pots
be sinister? I asked.

My dear she said *how could they not.*

So then as if by powerful compulsion she is suddenly out of bed is moving toward the windows. In the trees below she sees the mists that soon begin to take the form of people's shapes. They come together streaming toward the doorway down there seeping through that doorway in an evanescent chain.

The windows open out onto a darling little balcony.

She stands there

cheeks wet eyes in smears of blue no straps no cups legs shimmering sheerest

Under the impression that from life's sad circumstances she can finally hope to

I think I can feel within myself a little bit of what this room has seen so much of through the years.

But this sensation comes before the far more pressing realization that she still is lacking in so much of what she really needs.

She knows at last that this world

though it currently sees her all in velvet with a band of iridescent sequins mixed with opalescent beads with sea pearls interlacing with the beads

is not enough.

At first I felt the background penetrate the foreground.

I recalled the sweeping skies above the rolling hills.

I heard the glittering line between them snap.

My body weakened after that as if my body was a body now without the proper firmness as a cover for a soul that suddenly had lost its legs.

Wait!

Stop.

You say you would be interested in another story as a sequel to our previous subject whose strange origins I tried so awfully hard to trace?

A story of events occurring somewhere in a time behind this time?

Well she
the poor misguided figure
went careening in the night. The falling body outlined by the moon
bedazzled by the stars had been preceded by the teardrops pouring
from the window to the pavement. Like the icy waters of the sea that
pool of tears created as it does for all who contemplate such terrifying
jumps a nearly irresistible illusion of the timeless sympathetic even
comfy cozy destination down below.
For her
like others
Zillions.
who had gone before her but were now dispersed in particles accruing
in the sedimentary striations stacked in colors at the bottom of the sea
this was a choice. The opportunity to light upon a treasure trove of
jewels tucked in a corner. Roll about in the forgiving light of all the
gold the silver carved with meaningful engravings marking lineages
through generations.
Opportunity to sleep as angels do.
Blue heaven.
Angel of the deep.
The newest member of an endlessly enduring
How to get to there was what
as she so clearly understood
she had been looking for.

a world of watery chambers all connecting via countless waterhalls
communicated with by gentle waterlifts so delicately lit by incandes-
cent seashells
luminescent pearls

electric

darting

fishes

He
until there comes a time when he is able to resist
may feel so desperate to transport himself back into that long gone
boudoir to use his hand
to pick the overripened fruits up off the floor to put them back inside
that poor pathetic painting on the wall.
Each time he thinks of this however he will tell himself
as if in imitation of another
*Let us leave those for our neighbors. They can use them. We can't use
them anymore.*
Why not?

The walkway she said
double doors

Let go of me.

In other words
in life
as in the dream
already it's too late.